DEXTER'S LABORATORY™
SCIENCE LOG #3
WHAT'S THE "MATTER" WITH DEE DEE?

DEXTER'S LABORATORY™

SCIENCE LOG #3

WHAT'S THE "MATTER" WITH DEE DEE?

By Anne Capeci

Based on "DEXTER'S LABORATORY,"
as created by Genndy Tartakovsky

SCHOLASTIC INC.
New York   Toronto   London   Auckland   Sydney
Mexico City   New Delhi   Hong Kong   Buenos Aires

Visit us on the web at www.scholastic.com

No part of this publication may be
reproduced in whole or in part, or stored
in a retrieval system, or transmitted
in any form or by any means, electronic,
mechanical, photocopying, recording, or
otherwise, without written permission of the
publisher. For information regarding permission,
write to Scholastic Inc., Attention: Permissions
Department, 557 Broadway, New York, NY 10012.

ISBN 0-439-47240-7

Cover and interior illustrations by Francesc Mateu
Designed by Maria Stasavage

12 11 10 9 8 7 6 5 4 3 2 1   2 3 4 5 6 7/0
Printed in the U.S.A.
First printing, March 2003

Dexter's Laboratory™

SCIENCE LOG #3

WHAT'S THE "MATTER" WITH DEE DEE?

Chapter 1

"Dexter!" Dee Dee stood at the bottom of the stairs and called up to Dexter's bedroom.

Dexter, boy genius, was hard at work in the secret laboratory hidden behind his bookshelf. He was concentrating so hard on the work of Science that he barely heard his sister.

"For the last week I have worked to create my most advanced robot yet," he murmured to himself. "Now, at last, it is almost ready. The Dext-o-bot!"

A fiery blast of sparks shot from his blowtorch. Behind his protective helmet, Dexter's eyes shone with a wild intensity. He welded the robot's operating system into place. Then, throwing off his helmet, he began to make the last, precise adjustments.

"Just a few more turns of the microdriver, and —"

"Dex-ter!" Dee Dee called again.

Her voice was like a fly buzzing in his ear. Dexter's hand twitched in annoyance, causing him to turn the microdriver a fraction of a millimeter too far.

"Ooooooh!" Dexter fumed as he hurried to correct the mistake. "Only Dee Dee can manage to be such a pest without even being here in the laboratory! Why can't she show more respect for my important work? For my superior intelligence!"

Dee Dee was the only one in Dexter's family who knew about his secret laboratory. Dexter still didn't know how she had found out about it. But he did know that every time she interrupted him, he had to take precious time away from his critical scientific experiments.

"This time I will ignore her," he decided. He turned back to the Dext-o-bot. "Whatever she wants cannot be as important as —"

"DEX-TER!"

Dee Dee's voice shrieked into his ear. The shrill sound bounced off Dexter's eardrums and made him jump a foot and a half in the air.

When his boots hit the floor again, Dexter saw that Dee Dee was inside the laboratory now, and standing right next to him.

"What's the matter? Didn't ya hear me?" Dee Dee asked. She spun around in a pirouette. "Mom and Dad are waiting for you so we can go to the swim club for Mermaid Day. Come on!"

Dexter stared at her blankly. "Mermaid Day?" he repeated. The words meant nothing to him.

"Dex-ter!" Dee Dee scolded, putting her hands on her hips. "You know . . . Mermaid Day! A whole day of water games and activities? Not to mention a special mermaid water ballet with you-know-who as the star!"

Dee Dee made a flying ballet leap across the laboratory floor.

"Oh, brother." Dexter rolled his eyes. "Forget it, Dee Dee. I, Dexter, cannot just drop everything for your silly

splashing activities. Why should I go to a dumb swim club when everything I need for my important work of Science is right here?"

Dexter gazed proudly around his laboratory. It was a truly amazing place. He had filled it with powerful machines, spectacular robots, and ingenious formulas and inventions that he had created himself. Every time Dexter saw lights flashing on the control panel of his towering Computer, he couldn't help smiling.

This is where I belong, he thought.

"But everyone in town will be there!" Dee Dee argued. She kept leaping back and forth in front of him. "Besides, it's so hot out. Don't ya want to cool off?"

"I do not need a pool to keep cool," Dexter scoffed. "I can make my own cooling system in the blink of an eye. . . ."

As he spoke, Dexter scurried across the laboratory. He yanked open his supply cabinets and reached for tools and components. There was a frenzy of banging and assembling. Then . . .

"Aha!" Dexter held up a shiny metal machine that blew cold air out into the room. In his other hand was a high-tech air gun. When Dexter pulled the trigger, a cool blast of air shot toward Dee Dee. "See? I made not just one cooling system, but two of them!"

"Okay, okay. I get your point, Dexter," Dee Dee said.

But Dexter was on a roll. "I can make a dozen more, too. A thousand more!" he said.

Sliding both machines onto the floor, he reached for more wires and electronic programming cards. "Here is a voice-activated system . . . And this one here tells you the precise temperature and humidity level . . . even the molecular composition of the matter in the air. . . ."

He worked so quickly that all Dee Dee could see was a blur of moving hands and tools.

Machines piled up around them.

Beep!

Behind Dexter, lights flashed on Computer's control panel. Words scrolled across Computer's wide, sleek screen:

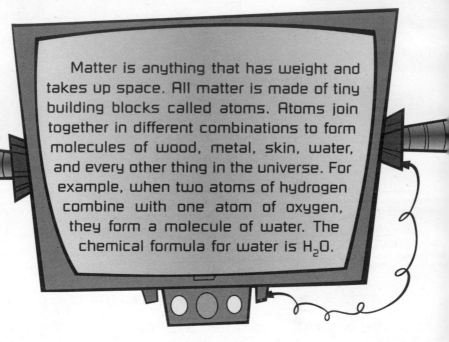

Matter is anything that has weight and takes up space. All matter is made of tiny building blocks called atoms. Atoms join together in different combinations to form molecules of wood, metal, skin, water, and every other thing in the universe. For example, when two atoms of hydrogen combine with one atom of oxygen, they form a molecule of water. The chemical formula for water is H_2O.

Dexter glanced at the report, but only for a moment. "Yes. Thank you, Computer," he said.

He turned back to yet another cooling system that he was assembling. This one was in the shape of his favorite superhero.

"Notice how Major Glory's muscles bulge when the cold air is turned on," he said. "And his eyes flash when . . ."

"What's this button for?" Dee Dee interrupted him. "Huh, Dexter?"

Dexter looked up from his Major Glory cooling system. Dee Dee was standing next to the mountain of machines he had tossed aside. In one hand she held the cooling gun Dexter had made. She

aimed it straight at herself, so that her pigtails and mermaid streamers blew in the chilly wind. With her other hand, Dee Dee pointed at a switch on the handle of the gun. As Dexter watched, she moved her finger closer to the button.

"That? That is the reverse button," Dexter told her. "Do not press it unless you want hot air to —"

Dee Dee pressed the button.

Dexter sighed. "Don't you ever listen?" he asked.

Whoooosh!

A blast of sizzling hot air shot from the gun. Even though Dexter was several feet away, beads of sweat dripped down his forehead.

"Wow! Those heat rays are more powerful than I thought!" he said.

Dee Dee's eyes popped wide open. Her face turned bright red, then purple. She opened her mouth to scream, but before she could . . .

Pop!

Dee Dee vanished into thin air!

Chapter 2

"Dee Dee!"

Dexter ran to where his sister had been. He waved his hands through the air, but felt nothing. His cooling gun had clattered to the floor. Dexter frowned down at it.

"My gun caused Dee Dee to . . . to self-destruct? But . . . how?" he wondered. He blew out a frustrated breath of air. "This is highly unscientific."

Beep!

A new report blinked onto Computer's screen:

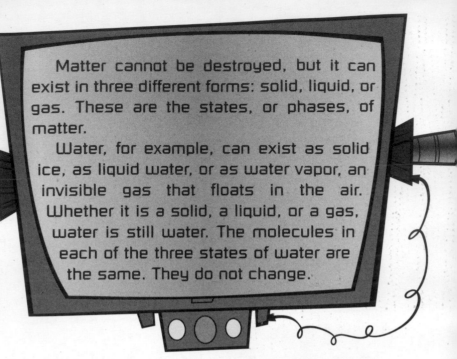

Matter cannot be destroyed, but it can exist in three different forms: solid, liquid, or gas. These are the states, or phases, of matter.

Water, for example, can exist as solid ice, as liquid water, or as water vapor, an invisible gas that floats in the air. Whether it is a solid, a liquid, or a gas, water is still water. The molecules in each of the three states of water are the same. They do not change.

"Of course!" Dexter perked up after reading the report. "Dee Dee has not self-destructed. Her molecules must have changed to a state of matter I cannot see, that is all."

He ran to his shiny chrome worktable and grabbed a pair of thick glass lenses. "Even if Dee Dee is in an invisible state," he said, "my megamolecular magnifying lenses will allow me to see the teeny-tiny molecules she is made of."

He snapped the lenses over his glasses and

gazed around the laboratory. "Now, let me see . . ."

The lenses magnified everything so much that his lab looked completely different. It was filled with ball-like atoms that were linked together as molecules. Dexter recognized atoms of oxygen in the air. He saw molecules of dust and . . .

"There!" he said, as an unusual combination of atoms came into view. "The Dee Dee molecule!"

There were hundreds of them . . . No, millions! Dee Dee molecules were all around Dexter,

floating in the laboratory.

Beep!

Dexter flipped up the magnifying lenses so he could read the new report that had just appeared on Computer's screen:

> Matter changes from one state to another when energy is added or taken away. Energy is what makes things move or change. Light, heat, sound, and electricity are all forms of energy.
>
> When heat energy is added to a substance, it makes atoms move more and spread out. As atoms spread out more and more, the substance changes from a solid to a liquid, and then from a liquid to a gas. When heat energy is removed from a substance — when it is cooled down instead of heated up — it changes from a gas to a liquid, and then from a liquid to a solid. When a substance changes into a gas, we say it evaporates.

"Hmmm . . ." Dexter flipped his mega-molecular magnifying lenses back down over his glasses so he could see the Dee Dee molecules once more.

PHASES OF MATTER

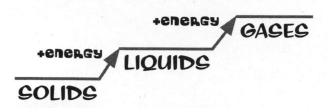

+ENERGY GASES

+ENERGY LIQUIDS

SOLIDS

"The reverse button on my cooling gun made Dee Dee heat up so much that she evaporated," he realized. "Dee Dee, you are a gas!"

The Dee Dee molecules in the air made no sound that Dexter could hear. They just wafted this way and that in the air. Dexter saw nothing to indicate that Dee Dee could hear him or respond.

"This is a first," Dexter said. He could not remember the last time his laboratory was so calm and quiet when his sister was in it. "Even though Dee Dee is hanging around, she cannot get in my way with her silly leaping and dancing. She cannot interrupt me with her dumb talk and stupid plans. Maybe it is not such a bad thing that she —"

"Dee Dee! Dexter!" Mom called from

downstairs. She sounded impatient. "Time to go!"

Dexter's whole body tensed. The swim club! He had forgotten all about it. *I must get Dee Dee back to normal before Mom comes looking for us!* he thought. *I cannot let her find my secret laboratory . . .*

"Um . . . We will be right there, Mother!" he shouted back.

Dexter knew he had to work fast. He snatched his cooling gun from the floor and pressed a switch on the handle. He tried to push it out of "Reverse" and back to "Normal Operation," but . . .

"Drat! It's jammed!"

Dexter reached frantically for his tools. "Monkey!" he called over his shoulder to his lab assistant. "I could use some assistance over here. . . ."

The only answer from Monkey's cage was a rumbling snore. Monkey lay sleeping with his hairy head resting on the floor of his cage.

"MONKEY!" Dexter said, louder this time. "NOW!"

Already, Dexter could hear footsteps on the stairs. Mom was coming! Panic shot through him like lightning.

"I must fix Dee Dee now!" he gasped. "If I do not, Mom will find my secret laboratory for sure!"

Chapter 3

"Here I am, Mother!" Dexter said a few moments later. "Er . . . I mean, here we are."

Dexter ran out of his bedroom. He had taken off his lab coat and changed into his swim trunks and flip-flops. Sweat ran down his forehead, but Dexter didn't wipe it away. He didn't dare let go of the life-size Dee Dee balloon he gripped by the hand.

Heh-heh-heh. Mom and Dad will never know the difference between the real Dee Dee and my Dee Dee balloon, he thought.

The Dee Dee balloon had pigtails, ballet slippers, and a tutu just like the real Dee Dee.

Dexter had drawn blue eyes and a dopey smile exactly like his sister's on the balloon's face. The Dee Dee balloon even had a recorded voice.

"Let us go to the swim club to partake of Mermaid Day activities," a flat, electronic voice said from Dee Dee's balloon mouth.

It was the best Dexter had been able to do. After all, he'd had less than a minute to make the balloon.

Mom was already halfway down the hall to Dexter's room. She stood watching them as Dexter yanked the Dee Dee balloon down the hallway.

The fake, rubbery Dee Dee bobbed and swayed. Dexter had stored all of the Dee Dee gas molecules inside the balloon. The gas was so light that it made the balloon float. Dexter had to keep a firm grip on the Dee Dee balloon's hand to keep its feet on the carpet.

"Dexter!" Mom said, looking horrified. She crossed her arms in front of her chest and frowned. "Look what you've done to your sister!"

Dexter skidded to a stop in front of Mom. He

glanced uneasily at the Dee Dee balloon. "D-done?" he asked.

"We're almost late for Dee Dee's water ballet, young man, and it's your fault," Mom said, wagging a finger at him.

Dexter breathed a sigh of relief. Mom thought the balloon was the real Dee Dee!

"Sorry, Mother . . ." Dexter hung his head, trying to look like he meant it. "It will not happen again. I promise."

Dexter did not give his mother a chance to say

anything else. He scrambled downstairs, pulling the Dee Dee balloon along with him. "Come on, Dee Dee," he said to the balloon. "Let us get into the car right away."

So far, so good, he thought.

Dexter glanced at the black belt pack that was strapped over his swim trunks. The Port-o-Lab waist pack. It contained vital elements from his laboratory — everything he needed to turn Dee Dee back into her normal self. Dexter had even brought along a video link to Computer!

Dexter was careful not to jostle the equipment as he ran outside to where Dad waited in the car. He shoved the Dee Dee balloon into the backseat ahead of him.

As soon as we get to the swim club, he thought, *I can use this to turn Dee Dee back into her normal self. I'll be back in my laboratory in no time!*

"Here we are!" Mom said cheerily as the car pulled into the swim club's parking lot.

"We've even got fifteen minutes to spare before your water ballet, Dee Dee," Dad said. He held his arm out so that his wristwatch was right in front of the Dee Dee balloon's painted face. "See?"

"Let us go to the swim club . . ." the balloon's electronic voice spoke up ". . . so we can partake of —"

Yikes! thought Dexter. *If I don't get away from Mom and Dad they're sure to catch on!* He began to yank the Dee Dee balloon away from his parents.

"I will take Dee Dee to, um, find the other mermaids," he said to them over his shoulder. "Yes — that is it! To find the other mermaids and get ready for the water ballet."

Keeping a firm hold on the balloon's puffed-out hand, Dexter hurried away from Mom and Dad. Behind his glasses, his eyes darted around uneasily.

The sun was impossibly bright. Blinding rays glinted off the water and made Dexter's head ache. Without his lab coat and clipboard, Dexter felt very uncomfortable. He had poured on the sunscreen, but he could almost hear his pale, sensitive skin cells crying out for relief from the burning sunshine.

"A superior scientific mind could fry to a crisp out here!" he grumbled.

Dexter frowned at the colorful "Welcome to Mermaid Day" banner. He scowled at the crowded bleachers that had been set up next to the pools. He glowered at the crowds of people that splashed in the pools, played on the grass, and crowded around the food hut.

"This noisy partaking of water fun is most inconvenient," he said. "It is so crowded that I, Dexter, see no place where I can work to restore Dee Dee's molecules to . . ."

Dexter stopped in mid-sentence. He squinted across the swim club at a pool he hadn't noticed before. Plywood panels painted with mermaid scenery had been set up all around it. Potted ferns and palm trees dotted the poolside area. Best of all, the pool had been roped off. A sign hanging from the rope said, "Closed until the Mermaid Water Ballet."

"Aha!" Dexter said. He pulled the Dee Dee balloon through the crowd to the pool and shoved it under the ropes. Then he scrambled behind a large panel decorated with colorful mermaids frolicking near an underwater castle.

Dexter sighed. "Not exactly optimum scientific conditions," he murmured to himself. "But it will have to do."

He tied the Dee Dee balloon to a palm branch. Unzipping his Port-o-Lab waist pack, he took out his miniature video link to Computer and strapped it around his wrist.

"Computer . . . activate!" he commanded.

The tiny screen lit up. It was already filled with information. Looking at the words, Dexter recognized part of the last report Computer had shown him before he had left his laboratory:

When heat energy is added to a substance, it makes atoms move more and spread out. As atoms spread out more and more, the substance changes from a solid to a liquid, and then from a liquid to a gas.

A gas is matter that has no shape or size of its own. That's because the atoms that make up gases are very active. They have much more energy than the atoms in solids or liquids. All that energy makes gas molecules really spread out and bounce around.

One of the special characteristics of a gas is that it will fill any container completely, instead of settling at the top or the bottom. As more gas is added, the gas molecules move closer together and the gas becomes more dense.

The report had given Dexter the idea to make the Dee Dee balloon in the first place. Dexter glanced at the puffed-out Dee Dee that was tied to the palm tree.

"The Dee Dee gas molecules fill the balloon completely, so there are no sagging parts," he mumbled. "But not for long!"

Dexter was already yanking tools and components from his Port-o-Lab waist pack. "I will change the Dee Dee gas molecules to a different phase and —"

Beep!

Dexter glanced at the new report that flashed on Computer's screen:

Did you know that water makes up about seventy percent of the human body?

"Excellent!" said Dexter. "So, if I change the Dee Dee molecules to their liquid state, Dee Dee will already be seventy percent back to normal! After that, a little fine-tuning will restore bones, muscles, skin, hair, and . . ."

Dexter shivered. He did not like to think about what, exactly, made up the other thirty percent of his sister.

". . . and all of the other stuff," he finished.

His brow was slick with sweat. The sun was blinding, and the sticky heat made it hard to handle his tools. Still, it took only a few moments for Dexter to put together his newest creation.

"At last! My new phase-changing gun is almost ready," he said, holding up the shiny metal machine. "With this, I, Dexter, will remove energy from the Dee Dee gas molecules so they will become liquid. All I have to do is test it and —"

At that moment, a dozen shrieking voices broke Dexter's concentration.

"Dee Dee! There you are!"

"We've been looking everywhere for you!"

"Where've you been?"

Dexter looked up and frowned.

A crowd of girls were scrambling past the rope

barrier. They ran toward the Dee Dee balloon.

"No!" Dexter stood in front of the Dee Dee balloon and waved his arms. "You must not — Hey! Watch it!"

He was nearly trampled as the girls stormed past him to Dee Dee.

"Time for our pre-ballet pep talk!" Dexter heard one of them squeal. "Mr. Manny wants everyone in the pool."

"Wait . . ." Dexter tried to grab the Dee Dee balloon away from them, but it was too late. The girls had already yanked the balloon free of the palm tree. As they carried Dee Dee to the pool, Dexter heard the balloon's electronic voice say, "Let us go to the swim club to partake of Mermaid Day activities."

Dexter groaned. "I've got to change the Dee Dee gas molecules to their liquid phase NOW!" he said.

There was no time to test the gun. Dexter squinted through the viewfinder to aim it. Sunlight glinted off the water. Dexter had to blink several times before he saw Dee Dee's water ballet friends and their coach, a man wearing shorts and a T-shirt with a whistle around his neck.

At last the Dee Dee balloon's phony face came into sight in the viewfinder of the phase-changing gun. The other girls were already pulling the balloon into the water.

Dexter didn't waste a nanosecond. He pulled the trigger.

ZZZZZZZAAAAAAAPPPPP!

All of a sudden, the girls' chattering voices fell

silent. Dexter felt a sudden chill in the air.

"Huh?" he murmured.

Dexter lowered the phase-changing gun. Right away he saw that the Dee Dee balloon had changed. It wasn't filled with gas anymore. Instead, it was stiff and hard, like a rock.

"Hmmm," said Dexter, frowning. "Liquid Dee Dee molecules should not make a stiff, hard shape. They should be wet and soupy inside the balloon."

But the Dee Dee molecules weren't the only things that had changed. As Dexter looked around, he saw that something had happened to the other mermaids, too. They were absolutely motionless. Mouths hung half-open, as if they had stopped in the middle of forming words. Arms and legs were bent in mid-jump. It was as if the girls had stopped suddenly when they were halfway in the pool. Mr. Manny stood rigid and still, too. Even the water in the pool had stopped moving!

Looking at it all, Dexter felt a sinking sensation in the pit of his stomach.

"Oh, no," he mumbled. "Do not tell me . . ."

He scrambled to the edge of the pool. The air there felt even cooler. When Dexter touched the water it was rock hard, and so cold that it stung his fingers.

"It's solid ice!" he realized.

He darted quickly toward the girls and Mr. Manny. One by one, he touched them. They, too, were absolutely stiff and very, very cold.

"I, Dexter, do not believe this," he groaned. "My phase-changing gun has made them all freeze solid!"

Chapter 4

Dexter ran over to the Dee Dee balloon. He ripped open its drooping, rubbery outside. Inside, a pile of tiny granules was heaped on the ground.

"Dee Dee? Is that you?" he said, squinting at the granules.

He thought he saw hints of pink and blue. Still, it was hard to imagine that this pile of . . . stuff was his sister.

Dexter dug into the Port-o-Lab waist pack, pulled out his mega-molecular magnifying lenses, and put them on.

"Ah! It is Dee Dee," he said.

There was no mistaking the familiar shape of the Dee Dee molecules. But there was something . . . different about them. The atoms that made up the molecules were much closer together than the atoms in the Dee Dee gas molecules. They were packed in so tightly that they didn't seem to move at all.

Dexter picked up one of the granules and rolled it between his fingers. "Wow! These things are as hard as rocks," he said.

Beep!

Dexter flipped up the magnifying lenses so he could look at the report that had appeared on his video link:

The atoms that make up solids do not have nearly as much energy as the atoms in liquids and gases. The atoms in liquids and gases can move in all directions. The atoms in solids can't. They are trapped in place and barely move at all. Because of this, solids have a very special characteristic. They hold their own shape. If you place a solid in a container, it won't change to fit the shape of the container. Even if you grind up a solid into a powder, the powder is made of tiny solids that don't change their shape.

When a substance changes into its solid state, we say that it freezes. The temperature at which a substance freezes is called its freezing point.

"So, the Dee Dee molecules are now solids!" Dexter said after reading the report.

He glanced at the unmoving figures of the other mermaids and Mr. Manny, and at the block of blue-green ice that filled the pool.

"Correction. Make that the Dee Dee molecules and everything they were touching when I shot the phase-changing rays," he added. "They have all frozen solid."

Dexter gazed thoughtfully at the shiny metal gun that he still clutched in his hand.

"I, Dexter, can only conclude that my phase-changing gun removed too much heat energy from Dee Dee's gas molecules. The gas cooled down so much, and so fast, that Dee Dee skipped the liquid phase and turned right into a solid!"

Dexter shrugged. "No big deal," he said. "It will take just a moment to readjust the phase-changer and —"

"Hey!" a loud voice broke into Dexter's thoughts. "Why is the pool still roped off?"

Dexter straightened up, listening. There were other voices, too, he realized. They sounded impatient — and very close by.

"The water ballet is supposed to start in five minutes," someone said.

"I want to get a good seat!" another person spoke up.

Dexter tiptoed to the edge of the mermaid

scenery. He peeked around and saw that some twenty people were pressed against the rope barrier. They looked as if they might burst into the pool area at any moment.

"Uh-oh," Dexter told himself. "I must hurry!"

He started back toward the mound of frozen Dee Dee molecules. He had taken only two steps when the toe of one flip-flop caught on the heel of the other . . .

"Whoa!"

Dexter flew forward. He threw his arms out, grabbing hold of the wooden scenery panel to keep his balance. The panel rocked unsteadily, then toppled over. Dexter jumped out of the way just in time.

Bam!

The huge wooden panel smashed down onto the frozen figures at the pool's edge. Dexter heard a noise that sounded like bits of broken glass cascading over the cement.

He peeked under the panel of scenery — and winced.

"This does not look good," he said.

Dexter didn't see Dee Dee's friends or Mr. Manny anymore. All he saw were heaps and heaps of frozen granules. The scenery panel had smashed the mermaids and Mr. Manny into bits!

"Dex-ter!"

The sound of Mom's voice made Dexter whirl around. Mom and Dad stood at the front of the crowd that waited to get inside the pool area. They did not look happy.

"Y-yes, Mother?" Dexter said.

"Why isn't the water ballet starting?" Mom asked. She looked puzzled and a little mad.

"Where are Dee Dee and all the other mermaids?" Dad asked.

Dexter did not like the curious way all those eyes were watching the pool area.

"Heh, heh, heh. Do not worry," he said, moving quickly to hoist the panel of scenery upright again. "They are just . . . uh, putting themselves together for the performance. It will only take me — I mean, them — a few more moments. I promise."

Dexter ran back behind the scenery panel before they could ask anymore questions.

As he went, he failed to notice a tall, thin boy who was watching him closely.

Chapter 5

Dexter's archenemy Mandark pushed his way to the front of the crowd waiting outside the pool. His beady eyes were locked on the spot where he'd just seen Dexter.

"No fair! How come Dork-ster gets to be with the mermaids and I don't?" Mandark complained.

Ever since he had arrived at the swim club, Mandark had been lurking outside the pool where the mermaid water ballet would take place. He was hoping to catch a glimpse of one mermaid in particular.

"Dee Dee," he murmured in a dreamy voice.

Just thinking about her made Mandark's heart beat louder in his chest. "If only I could be near her . . ."

His eyes darted left, then right. Moving quickly and quietly, Mandark slipped beneath the rope barrier. He tiptoed past  the wooden scenery panels and ducked down next to a potted palm tree near the pool.

Peeking out from behind the pot, he searched the pool area for Dee Dee.

Hmmm. No sign of her, thought Mandark.

But what he did see made him very confused.

"The pool is filled with ice, not water," he said, frowning. "Why? And what is all of that . . ." He stared at the mountains of granules that were heaped around the pool. ". . . that stuff?"

Mandark's eyes flew to Dexter. He was instantly suspicious. "You are up to something — I know it!" he murmured. "But . . . what?"

Dexter was pulling tools from a belt pack he wore over his swim trunks. Mandark couldn't get a clear look at the shiny silver machine Dexter was working on. Dexter muttered to himself while he worked, and Mandark strained to hear his words.

". . . frozen molecules . . . must restore . . . get Dee Dee back to normal . . ."

Mandark didn't need to hear anymore. *My beloved Dee Dee is . . . frozen!* he realized.

"This is all your fault, Dork-ster," Mandark said

under his breath. "I, Mandark, will make you pay for what you've done to Dee Dee."

"Ready!" Dexter tucked his tools back inside the Port-o-Lab waist pack, then held the phase-changing gun carefully in his hands. "And not a moment too soon!"

He checked his watch. It had taken him just fifty-seven seconds to readjust the phase-changing gun. But the crowd outside the pool sounded louder and more impatient than ever!

"This time," Dexter went on, "my phase-changing gun will add the precise amount of energy needed to change the frozen molecules to their liquid state. . . ."

ZZZZZAAAAAP!

Dexter shot the phase-changing gun at the frozen ice in the pool.

ZZZZAAAAAPPPPPPP!

He fired it at the mountains of frozen granules that lay on the ground.

ZAP! ZAAAPPP! ZZZAAAAPPPPPPP!

He didn't stop until he had fired the gun at every single frozen solid particle he could see. Only then did he lower the gun.

"Yes!" Dexter crowed.

The ice in the pool had melted to water that splashed gently to and fro. The piles of granules had turned into a mess of liquid puddles that spread out on the cement around the pool. Dexter spotted dozens of colors swirling around one another.

"Looks like mermaid soup to me!" he said. He dropped the gun in the grass and ran over for a closer look. "Dee Dee, all the other mermaids, and Mr. Manny have changed phases, just as I planned. They are liquids!"

Beep!

Computer's signal alerted Dexter to a new report that appeared on the screen of his video link:

Liquids contain more energy than solids, but less energy than gases. That means that the atoms and molecules that make up liquids move around some, but not nearly as much as the atoms and molecules in gases.

Liquids have some unique characteristics. A liquid will take the shape of any container you put it in, but it doesn't fill the whole container at once. Gravity causes the liquid to fill the bottom first, and then the rest. Once a container is full, you cannot squeeze in any more liquid. That's because liquids do not compress easily — you cannot squeeze them into a smaller space. (Gases, on the other hand, can be squeezed closer together.)

When a solid changes to a liquid, we say that it melts. The temperature at which this happens is called its melting point.

"No wonder this liquid mermaid soup is sloshing all over the cement," Dexter said after reading the report. "The liquids don't have a container to fill up, so they are just spreading out all over."

Dexter squinted at the puddles, but he couldn't begin to tell which parts of the liquid belonged to his sister.

"The Dee Dee molecules are all mixed up with molecules from her friends and Mr. Manny. But no matter," he said, shrugging. "That is not a problem for a boy of my scientific talents. . . ."

Dexter hurried back to where he had left the phase-changing gun on the grass. "It is just a question of fine-tuning," he went on. "I, Dexter, will separate the molecules and restore everyone to their original form in the blink of an —"

He stopped short and stared down at the grass. It was flat and matted down where he had dropped the gun. But the gun itself was no longer there.

"That is odd," Dexter said, frowning. "I left it right here!"

He turned in every direction, looking frantically

around the pool area. He looked behind palm trees and under towels. He looked on lawn chairs and behind the shower, in the pool cabana and under beach umbrellas. But it was no use.

The phase-changing gun was gone.

Chapter 6

"Ha-ha-ha! Ha-ha-ha-ha-ha!" Mandark cackled to himself as he tiptoed away from the roped-off pool. "I, Mandark, have really outsmarted that pipsqueak Dexter this time. I snatched this . . ." he patted the bulge in his lab coat where Dexter's phase-changing gun was hidden ". . . right from under his nose, and Dork-ster never even saw me!"

How Mandark had enjoyed seeing the look of panic on Dexter's face when he realized that the gun was gone! Mandark had been tempted to stick around to watch Dexter squirm. But he had something better to do.

"This is just the beginning," Mandark gloated. "While Dexter is trying to find his dumb gun, I will be attacking my enemy where it will hurt him the most. . . ."

For once, Dexter was not in his laboratory. Mandark would be able to destroy all of his equipment and inventions — his whole laboratory! — and Dexter wouldn't even know about it until it was too late.

Just before Mandark reached the swim club exit, he paused. He wanted to leave, but something held him back. His feelings for Dee Dee.

"I will be back soon," he promised, glancing back at the roped-off pool. "Then I will finish the job that Dexter botched. I will restore my beloved Dee Dee to her beautiful, perfect self."

Getting into Dexter's lab was easier than it ever

had been before. Mandark had no trouble disabling Dexter's useless security devices. He didn't even have to be quiet or sneaky!

"Ha-ha-ha! Ha-ha-ha-ha-ha!" Mandark walked right into the middle of Dexter's laboratory. His beady eyes took in everything — Dexter's high-tech robots, the voice-activated surface skimmer, Dexter's deep freeze, his molecular fusion tank, and his towering, gleaming Computer. . . .

Mandark cackled with glee when he saw Monkey still sound asleep, snoring in his cage.

"This is going to be even simpler than I expected. Time to get to work!" Mandark pulled the phase-changing gun from beneath his lab coat. "And I know just where to start. . . . "

He held out the shiny gun and aimed it at Computer.

"Where is it?" Dexter mumbled. He raced up and down the cement area surrounding the roped-off pool. "WHERE?"

Precious seconds had elapsed. Dee Dee, the other mermaids, and their coach were still a big soupy mess of liquid molecules. Dexter tried not to step on them as he searched madly for his phase-changing gun.

It was getting harder to concentrate on his search. The crowd waiting for the water ballet had grown larger. Angry voices joined together, getting louder and louder.

"WE . . . WANT . . . THE . . . WATER . . .

BALLET!" the voices chanted in unison. "WE . . . WANT . . . THE . . . WATER . . . BALLET!"

Dexter hid as far behind the mermaid panels as he could. "This situation is getting out of control!" he murmured.

"Computer! Monkey!" Dexter spoke urgently into his video link. "I need back up here! Can you tell me where my . . . "

At that moment, Dexter saw something move on the screen of his video link. Something had popped up right in front of Computer's screen.

"Monkey?" Dexter said.

But whatever was in front of Computer didn't have hairy arms or a dark, furry head. Instead, Dexter saw a tall, gangly figure wearing glasses and a white lab coat.

"Mandark!" he growled. "What are YOU doing in MY laboratory? Get out immediately!"

"Fat chance . . . Dork-ster," Mandark's nasal voice came through Dexter's video link.

Dexter gasped when he saw the shiny silver gun in Mandark's hands. "So that is why I cannot find

my phase-changing gun," he said. "You took it!"

"Ha-ha-ha! Ha-ha-ha-ha-ha!" Mandark let out a smug, evil laugh. Then he aimed the phase-changing gun at Computer and pulled the trigger.

"NOOOOOOOOOOO!" Dexter shouted.

But there was nothing Dexter could do. Computer dissolved into a shiny silver liquid that spread out all over the laboratory floor.

Chapter 7

Dexter could hardly breathe. He gaped at the silver liquid he saw on the video link.

"You've . . . you've . . . melted Computer!" he cried.

Mandark did not bother to respond. He pointed the phase-changing gun at Dexter's deep freeze.

ZZZAAAAAAPPPPPPPPP!!!!

All Dexter could do was stare in horror at the screen of the video link. In a flash, his deep freeze turned into a dripping, liquid mess. It was like his worst nightmare coming true before his eyes.

"Monkey! HELP!" Dexter shouted. "You must

get rid of Mandark . . . before he liquifies my entire laboratory!"

The video link did not show all of Dexter's laboratory. Dexter could not see Monkey's cage. But the sounds of snoring told Dexter what his lab assistant was doing.

Dexter sighed. "Must I do everything myself? I've got to get back to the lab right away!"

He barely glanced at the liquid soup of Dee Dee, the other mermaids, and Mr. Manny. All Dexter could think about was getting Computer, and his laboratory, out of Mandark's evil clutches . . . FAST.

Dexter zipped the Port-o-Lab waist pack shut, and then raced from the pool.

At least, he *tried* to.

He was stopped cold by the wall of people waiting to get into the pool area.

"WE . . . WANT . . . THE . . . WATER . . . BALLET!" they shouted.

Dexter screeched to a halt just in front of them. "Heh, heh, heh . . ."

He looked for a way out. No matter which way he turned, people blocked his way. They all stared at him with angry, impatient faces.

"Dex-ter!" Mom said. Her face was red and sweaty. Next to her, Dad looked annoyed, too.

"What's going on, son?" he asked.

Dexter's eyes darted nervously left, then right. "I, um . . ." he began.

At that moment, he caught sight of the food hut. It was clear across the swim club — far from the pool where the water ballet was supposed to take place.

"LOOK!" Dexter shouted, pointing in the direction of the hut. "There's FREE ICE CREAM at the food hut! NOW!!!"

A hundred faces turned to look at the food hut. A moment later, the ground shook as everyone stormed toward it. People elbowed one another out of the way, trying to get to the free ice cream first.

Dexter was the only one left standing near the roped-off pool.

"Yes!" he crowed.

Dexter knew his distraction wouldn't keep people away from the pool for long. But at least there was a clear path to the exit now. He ran toward it, heading for home as fast as his legs would take him.

"I cannot worry about Dee Dee and the other mermaids now," he said. "Not until I stop Mandark from destroying my laboratory!"

It took him almost ten minutes to get home. Dexter ran so fast that he had to gasp for air as he pushed through the front door and raced upstairs to his bedroom.

Dexter frowned when he saw his bookshelf pushed up to reveal the secret entrance to his laboratory.

"Mandark must still be there," he muttered under his breath. "That sneak!"

Clenching his teeth together, Dexter ran through the doorway — and then stopped short.

"Oh, no . . . " he breathed.

His laboratory was in a shambles. "My deep-freeze . . . my remote-control surface skimmer . . . my Dext-o-bot!" he cried. "All of my greatest inventions have been . . . liquified!"

All that was left of them were a series of shiny metallic puddles. The thick liquids dripped from his worktables and shelves. Puddles swirled into one another on the laboratory floor.

Dexter picked his way across the puddles to the

very center of the lab. There, where Computer had once stood so tall, an enormous lake of silver liquid oozed across the floor. Dexter's phase-changing gun lay next to it.

"Computer . . ." Dexter said, choking back a sob.

Then, as he stepped past one of his worktables, Dexter spotted his enemy. Mandark was crouched next to the shiny silver puddle of liquified Computer. In his hand was a test tube that contained a milky substance Dexter didn't recognize.

"Hold it right there, Mandark!" Dexter commanded.

Mandark's eyes gleamed with triumph. "It's a good thing you're wearing your swim trunks," he said. "Once I'm done with your laboratory, the only thing it will be good for is swimming!"

Dexter heard a faint gurgling sound coming from the puddle of silver liquid on the floor. As Dexter watched, it bubbled slightly. Then a faint, watery beep sounded from Dexter's video link.

"I think Computer is trying to communicate with me!" Dexter said.

He glanced at the tiny screen — and blinked in surprise. A report had appeared on the screen!

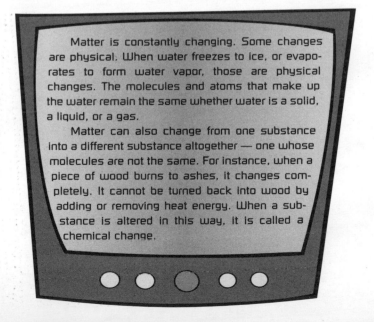

Matter is constantly changing. Some changes are physical. When water freezes to ice, or evaporates to form water vapor, those are physical changes. The molecules and atoms that make up the water remain the same whether water is a solid, a liquid, or a gas.

Matter can also change from one substance into a different substance altogether — one whose molecules are not the same. For instance, when a piece of wood burns to ashes, it changes completely. It cannot be turned back into wood by adding or removing heat energy. When a substance is altered in this way, it is called a chemical change.

"You are really something, Computer," Dexter said, shaking his head in amazement. "Even as a liquid, you are able to function better than most humans! But . . ." He frowned down at the screen of his portable video link. "Why are you telling me about chemical changes of matter? Unless . . ." Dexter whirled around to face Mandark. He glowered at the beaker in Mandark's hand.

"Don't tell me you are planning to make a chemical change — a chemical change to Computer?" Dexter said.

A sickening smile spread across Mandark's face. "You guessed it, Dork-face," he said. "One tiny drop of this formula will alter Computer's chemical makeup. Computer will be destroyed for good!"

"NO! I, Dexter, will NOT allow it," Dexter said firmly.

In a flash, he made a dive for the phase-changing gun. As soon as his hands closed around the handle, he scrambled to his feet and aimed the gun at Mandark. He reached for the trigger, but before he could pull it . . .

"Take that, Dexter!" Mandark said.

Holding the beaker right over the puddle of silver liquid, he tilted it. A single milky droplet slipped over the edge of the beaker and fell toward the silver lake of Dexter's beloved, liquified Computer.

Chapter 8

"No! You will NOT succeed," cried Dexter. "Not this time . . ."

Moving with supersonic speed, Dexter grabbed a screwdriver from his Port-o-Lab waist pack. Out of the corner of his eye, he saw the droplet of Mandark's formula. It was falling closer and closer to the silver soup of Computer's molecules.

"Ha-ha-ha!" Mandark's triumphant laugh filled the air.

Dexter gritted his teeth and worked even faster. He made a lightning-quick adjustment to the phase-changing gun. Then he carefully aimed it at the droplet and pulled the trigger.

ZZZAAAAAAAPPPPPPPPP!

Dexter held his breath. Was he too late? The droplet of formula was so close to Computer — it was almost on top of the silvery surface!

Pop!

The droplet vanished before it could plop down into the silver liquid.

"Computer!" Dexter called. "Are you all right?"

The silver liquid bubbled, and Dexter heard a faint, unsteady beep. He looked quickly down at his video link and saw a few words on the screen:

All sectors are operational, Dexter.

Dexter's whole body drooped with relief.

"Ha! I, Dexter, have added enough heat energy to your dumb formula to make it evaporate into a gas!" he told Mandark. "The tiny molecules are so light that they are floating up into the air . . . away from Computer!"

"What?!" Mandark scowled at Dexter. "Well,

there's more formula where that came from," he said.

Mandark turned the test tube of milky formula upside down. This time, Dexter was ready for him.

ZZZZZZAAAAAPPPPPPPPPPP!!!!

Dexter shot his phase-changing gun at the beaker.

ZZZZZZZAAAAAAAPPPPPPPPPPP!!!!!

He blasted the gun at Mandark.

The next thing he knew, Mandark and his beaker of formula disappeared from sight. "Now Mandark

is a gas, too!" Dexter said. "At least, I think he is."

Dexter took his mega-molecular magnifying lenses from his Port-o-Lab waist pack and snapped them onto his glasses. Sure enough, Mandark molecules wafted through the air as a gas, alongside gas molecules of the formula.

"Perfect," Dexter said with a grin. "Now Mandark is such a lightweight scientist that he cannot do anything more to hurt Computer or destroy my laboratory."

Dexter was pleased with his work. But he wasn't done yet!

"Monkey!" he called. His flip-flops slapped against the floor as he hurried to his assistant's cage. "There is much to do!"

Monkey continued to snore softly in his cage.

He looked as if he hadn't budged all day.

"Some help you've been," Dexter grumbled.

He was annoyed with his lab assistant, but there wasn't time to give Monkey a lecture.

"I must return to the swim club," he said. "If I don't fix Dee Dee and the other mermaids soon, there will be a riot!"

Chapter 9

"Ahhhhhhhh!" said Dexter. "At last, everything is back to normal . . . thanks to Science."

He glanced around the pool area. Without Mandark's interference, Dexter's phase-changing gun had worked perfectly! It had been easy for Dexter to change Dee Dee and the other mermaids back to their normal selves. Now they were in the pool, warming up for their ballet while spectators found seats in the bleachers. Mr. Manny, the girls' coach, stood next to the pool, calling out directions as they glided and splashed through the water. Much to Dexter's relief, none of them seemed to remember a thing about what had happened to them.

"Oh, Dex-ter!" Dee Dee called to him.

Dexter left his phase-changing gun and tools in a heap on the cement. When he got to the edge of the pool, Dee Dee was swimming in a circle.

"Admit it, Dexter," she said. "You're glad you came to Mermaid Day. Aren't you?"

Dexter did not answer. He was dy-ing to get back to his lab-oratory, but he didn't think Dee Dee would un-derstand. After all, he could not expect in-ferior minds like hers to understand true scien-tific genius.

"See?" Dee Dee waved toward the crowded

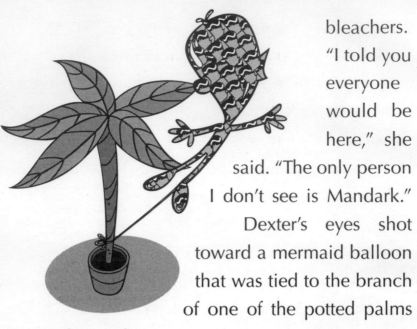

bleachers. "I told you everyone would be here," she said. "The only person I don't see is Mandark."

Dexter's eyes shot toward a mermaid balloon that was tied to the branch of one of the potted palms next to the pool.

"Do not worry, Dee Dee — I am sure Mandark is, um, floating around here somewhere," he said.

Dexter had stored Mandark's gas molecules inside the balloon. Even though his archenemy was a gas, Dexter still did not trust him. He wanted to be sure Mandark stayed where he could keep an eye on him.

"Look! Even Monkey came!" Dee Dee squealed.

Dexter could not believe his eyes. Monkey was there. He swung toward the bleachers on his long, hairy arms. Dexter started toward him.

"Monkey! Could you not have ended your nap a little earlier?" Dexter scolded when he caught up to his lab assistant. "You are far too late to be of any real help to me now."

Monkey did not appear to be disturbed by this news. He stopped to peel a banana, and then popped it into his mouth.

"No matter. You can still make yourself useful," Dexter went on. "Pick up my phase-changing gun and tools, Monkey. We must return to the laboratory immediately. Computer is still waiting to be restored to its optimum performance!"

Dexter waited until he saw

Monkey pick up the phase-changing gun in his hairy hand. Then he started toward the swim club exit.

"DEX-TER!" Dee Dee's voice called after him. "You're not LEAVING, are you?" she said.

Dexter did not bother to turn around or answer her. "Of course I am leaving," he muttered under his breath. "My work here is done. Important chores await me in my laboratory. I cannot stick around to watch —"

ZZZZAAAAAAAAAPPPP!

Dexter heard the hum of the phase-changing gun. A warm, tingling feeling shot through him from head to toe.

"Oooooooh," he said, blinking. "Why do I feel so. . . . light-headed?"

"Yeah! Bravo!" Mom and Dad shouted from the bleachers.

They watched proudly as Dee Dee and the other mermaids formed a twirling star in the pool.

"That's my girl!" Dad exclaimed.

Dexter was with them, too. He was rising up toward the stands, with Monkey holding on tight to him. He looked oddly puffed out, and the expression on his face was stiff — as if it had been drawn on with crayons. Dexter's arms and legs stuck out strangely, and he kept floating upward into the air. Monkey yanked Dexter downward and patted Dexter's puffy hands together to make them clap.

Mom and Dad looked at each other and smiled.

"Isn't it sweet?" Mom said. "Dexter is so happy to see Dee Dee's water ballet that he's practically floating on air!"

Next to them, Monkey just laughed.

THE END